For
Teun & Josephine

First published in the UK in 2018 by Lemniscaat Ltd, Kemp House, 152 City Road, London EC1V 2NX
Distributed worldwide by Thames & Hudson, 181A High Holborn, London WC1V 7QX

ISBN 13: 978-1-78807-016-4 (Hardcover)
Printing and binding: Graphius, Gent
First UK edition

www.lemniscaat.co.uk

Daphne Louter LOOK, RABBITS

LEMNISCAAT